Grimm's Fairy Tales

Retold from the classic originals
by Deanna McFadden

Illustrated by Eric Freeberg

STERLING

New York / London
www.sterlingpublishing.com/kids

STERLING and the distinctive Sterling logo
are registered trademarks of Sterling Publishing Co., Inc.

Library of Congress Cataloging-in-Publication Data

McFadden, Deanna.
 Grimm's fairy tales / retold from the classic originals by Deanna McFadden ;
illustrated by Eric Freeberg.
   v. cm. — (Classic starts)
 Contents: The tale of the boy who learned fear—Little brother and little sister—
Rapunzel—Hansel and Grethel—Cinderella—Briar Rose—Snow White—
Rumpelstiltskin—The golden goose—The worn-out dancing shoes—The brave
little tailor.
 ISBN 978-1-4027-7311-2
 1. Fairy tales—Germany. [1. Fairy tales. 2. Folklore—Germany.] I. Freeberg, Eric, ill.
II. Grimm, Jacob, 1785–1863. III. Grimm, Wilhelm, 1786–1859. IV. Title.
 PZ8.M175965Gr 2011
 398.20943—dc22
 [E]

                                                                                  2010016438

Lot#:
8 10 9
02/17
Published by Sterling Publishing Co., Inc.
387 Park Avenue South, New York, NY 10016
Text © 2011 by Deanna McFadden
Illustrations © 2011 by Eric Freeberg
Distributed in Canada by Sterling Publishing
$^c/_o$ Canadian Manda Group, 165 Dufferin Street
Toronto, Ontario, Canada M6K 3H6
Distributed in the United Kingdom by GMC Distribution Services
Castle Place, 166 High Street, Lewes, East Sussex, England BN7 1XU
Distributed in Australia by Capricorn Link (Australia) Pty. Ltd.
P.O. Box 704, Windsor, NSW 2756, Australia

Classic Starts is a trademark of Sterling Publishing Co., Inc.

Printed in China
All rights reserved

Sterling ISBN 978-1-4027-7311-2

For information about custom editions, special sales, premium and
corporate purchases, please contact Sterling Special Sales
Department at 800-805-5489 or specialsales@sterlingpublishing.com.

CONTENTS

CHAPTER 1

The Tale of the Boy Who Learned Fear

∽

There once lived a man who had two sons. The older boy was smart and very good at his chores. The younger boy was very strong but had trouble learning. Sometimes the man would ask his older son to fetch something in the dark or walk into town through the graveyard. The older boy always said, "Oh no, Father, I couldn't. I'm just too afraid!" He was *terrified* of dark, spooky places. The younger son was not.

While the man loved both of his sons, he

never asked the younger boy for help with chores. The boy always made a mess of things.

"What am I going to do with you?" his father would say.

In the evenings, the neighborhood would gather to tell scary stories around a fire. The tales were so scary that they sent chills up and down the spines of all who listened. The boy listened, too. He noticed that all his neighbors—including his brother and father—would shudder during the scariest parts of the stories. They cried, "Oh, that makes me shudder!"

The boy couldn't figure out what this meant. He wondered, *Why do they all shudder?*

Then the boy had an idea. He thought, *Maybe that's what I need to do. I need to learn how to shudder like my brother. He always does everything right.*

Many months passed. Still the boy wondered why everyone, except for him, knew how to shudder. He grew taller and his shoulders grew wider. Still, he couldn't figure it out.

One day, his father said to him, "Son, you are growing up. Soon, you'll be a man. You need to learn a trade. You have seen how hard your older brother works."

"Father," the son said, "I would love to learn a trade. But first, I think I need to learn how to shudder. Everyone knows how except me."

His older brother laughed. "You are too foolish for your own good. You'll never amount to anything."

Their father sighed. "Even if you figure out how to shudder, that will not put bread on your table, my son."

"What am I going to do with you?" his father said to his son. The young man shrugged.

The next day, the father said, "Do you truly want to learn to shudder? Then you should set off into the world all alone. That is the best way. But you must not tell anyone who you are or where you come from. You are a young man now, strong enough to take care of yourself. I forbid you to ask for help. You must be completely alone. It's the only way you'll learn to shudder."

He gave his son a little bit of money and wished him well. Soon the young man was walking down the road all by himself. *If only I could shudder, then I could go home again,* he said to himself.

The young man walked into an inn to spend the night. He asked for a room. The innkeeper asked, "What's a young man like you doing out this way all by yourself?"

The young man replied, "I'm trying to learn how to shudder."

The innkeeper laughed. "Is that all? Well, I can certainly help you."

The innkeeper's wife looked at her husband and said, "I know what you're thinking right now. Do not send this young man to that haunted castle!"

"But I want to learn how to shudder," the young man said, sighing. "Please tell me."

The innkeeper told him the haunted castle wasn't far away. "If you can last three nights there, the king of this land will reward you. He has great treasure, and he is also willing to offer his daughter's hand in marriage."

The young man said, "Treasure and a pretty princess aren't important to me. I just want to learn how to shudder."

The innkeeper continued, "Evil spirits guard the haunted castle where the king's riches are hidden. The king himself used to live there. But a witch cast a spell on the castle. It can only be broken if one brave person can last through three nights in the spooky place."

The innkeeper's wife added, "Many have tried. All have run away scared after a few hours."

The next day, the young man stood before the king. He asked for a chance to spend three nights in the haunted castle. The king looked at him for a long time, then gave him permission. He said, "You may take five objects with you. What shall they be?"

The young man thought for a moment, then replied, "I will need matches and wood for a fire. I would like a tool for cutting the wood if it's too big for the fireplace. And I will need a woodcarver's bench with a good knife."

The king's servants brought the objects to the young man. They walked him to the haunted castle and then left, whispering to one another, "He will not even last the night."

When night fell, the young man made a fire to keep warm. He sat down on his bench and thought, *I can't see anything in this old castle that could make me shudder.*

Midnight came. The young man poked at the fire and yawned. Two huge black cats crept out of the shadows and meowed, "We are freezing to death."

"Silly cats," the young man said. "I didn't see you there. Come to the fire and get warm."

They hissed as they jumped forward. "Do you want to play a game?" they asked. Their eyes were fiery red.

"First, show me your paws." The young man looked at the size of their claws and said, "I'm not playing with the pair of you."

Before either cat could scratch him, he grabbed them and tossed them outside. Then he sat down by the fire. Suddenly cats and dogs with fiery eyes came out of every corner. They moaned, groaned, and stomped on his fire. The young man became angry.

"Enough!" he shouted. "It's cold and you are making it colder. Stay away from my fire!"

The cats and dogs had never seen anyone who wasn't scared of them. They scurried away, suddenly afraid. Once they were gone, the young man built up his fire. He grew sleepy, so he crawled into the giant bed in the corner.

But the moment he closed his eyes, the bed started shaking! The bed lifted off the ground and flew all around the castle. The young man laughed. "Keep going!" he shouted. "What fun!"

The bed flew through doors and bumped up and down the stairs. Boom! Crash! It turned upside down and landed on top of him. The young man pulled himself from under the bed and said, "What a great ride!"

All the excitement made the young man tired. He tugged the blanket and pillow from the overturned bed. Then he lay down on his bench and fell asleep.

The next morning, the king expected to find the young man in a terrible state of fright.

When the king looked through the window, he saw the young man lying on the bench.

He said, "What a shame! This handsome young man didn't even make it through the first night."

The young man woke up as the king spoke. "Wait a minute," he said. "I'm still here! I was just sleeping."

"How did you do it?" the king asked, shocked.

"It wasn't hard at all. I made a fire, tossed out some nasty cats and dogs, went for a ride on a bed, and fell asleep. I didn't shudder even once." The young man stretched. "But there are two more nights to go."

Night fell again. The fire roared. Terrible sounds came from all directions. Suddenly there was a horrible cry. An awful pale, thin ghost slid down the chimney. He landed right in front of the young man.

The young man stood up and said to the

ghost, "You seem to be shivering. Come and sit with me by the fire."

The ghost tried to take the young man's bench. "No, you need to sit over here," the young man said. He pushed the ghost onto the floor. Suddenly the room started to shake and rumble. In an instant many more ghosts appeared. They were all carrying bags of skulls and bones.

"Hurrah!" the young man said. "Let's use these old bones to have a bowling game."

The young man and the ghosts quickly set up the game. They had a grand old time. When the clock struck midnight, the ghosts disappeared. The young man went to sleep for the night.

Once again, the king found the young man in the haunted castle in the morning. "What happened last night?" he asked.

The young man replied, "We had a terrific bowling game! It was a fun time, even if the other players didn't talk much."

The king was amazed. "Let's see how tonight goes."

"I hope I finally learn to shudder. This will be my last night in the castle," the young man replied.

The third night came. A little before midnight, the young man sat down on his bench and said, "If only I could find *something* to make me shudder."

At that very moment, an old man with a long white beard entered the room. He said, "If you don't pass my test, young man, you will surely die. Follow me."

He led the young man down many dark hallways filled with cobwebs. Finally they came to an old door. Behind the door was an ax and iron block.

"If you can prove you are stronger than I am, I will let you live," the old man said.

The young man laughed. "I am very strong.

I always have been. Look at the size of my shoulders!"

"Can you do this?" With the ax, the old man sliced into the iron block with one stroke.

"Is that all?" the young man asked. "Watch." He pulled the ax out of the block. He swung it high above his head. As it came crashing down, it broke the iron block into two pieces.

The old man was surprised. "No one has ever been strong enough to pass this test. I will let you live. Now you must come with me."

They passed through another dark hallway. Stopping at another door, the old man raised his bony finger. He said, "You spent three nights facing terrible things, and you survived. You have broken the spell on the king's haunted castle."

The old man opened the door. Behind it were three chests of treasure.

"One chest for the poor," he said. "Another belongs to the king. The last one is yours."

"Thank you for showing me the treasure," the boy said. "I am glad I could break the spell for the king. But the treasure is not important to me. All I wanted was to learn how to shudder."

The clock struck midnight, and the old man disappeared without another word. The young man shrugged. He thought, *It is dark here, but I think I can find my way back to my warm room.*

He felt his way along cold walls covered in spiderwebs. Finally, he found the room where he had left the fire burning. The young man fell asleep by the fire. Again the king found him the next morning.

"You have broken the spell on my castle," the king said. "You have saved my kingdom. You may marry my daughter."

"I am pleased that I have broken the terrible spell for you. And I will gladly marry your daughter. But I still don't know how to shudder."

The king brought the young man back to his

castle. There he met the princess. She was lovely and kind. Their wedding was celebrated by the entire kingdom. The young man was very happy, even though he never learned to shudder.

The young man honored the old ghost's words and gave one of the treasure chests to the poor. The king was pleased to have his chest of treasure back. He used it to fix up the castle that was no longer haunted.

I'm very lucky, the young man thought. *My father was right. I did need to go out on my own to make my way in the world. But he was wrong about one thing—I still haven't learned how to shudder.*

Many years went by, and eventually the young man became king. But it still bothered him that he had never learned to shudder. He talked about it all the time to his wife, the queen. The queen got very annoyed with hearing him complain about this silly thing. She formed a plan. Late one night, she filled up a bucket with cold water and slimy fish. The young king was fast asleep.

The queen pulled back the blankets and dumped the bucket on her sleeping husband. The cold water shocked him awake. The little fish wriggled all over his skin. The young king jumped out of bed and shuddered like crazy. The slimy fish had done the trick.

"My dear wife, you've done it!" he said, hopping and shuddering around the bedroom. "I have finally learned how to shudder! Now help get these slimy fish off me in a hurry."

CHAPTER 2

Little Brother and Little Sister

❦

One morning, Little Brother took Little Sister's hand and said, "Our lives have been so hard ever since our mean stepmother and her ugly, one-eyed daughter came to live with us. She makes us eat stale bread. She forces us to do all the chores. Our stepsister sits around doing nothing! We need to leave home and find our own way in the world."

"You are right. What else can we do?" Little Sister said. "But if she ever catches us, it will be the end of us both."

"It's a chance that we have to take," Little Brother said.

The pair left home that day. They had only the clothes on their backs. By nightfall, they reached the edge of a great forest. Little Brother looked up at the tall trees and said, "We can hide safely in here for the night." He crawled into the bottom of a hollow old tree.

Little Sister followed him inside the tree. Soon the pair were asleep. The bright sun woke them up the next morning. As they stepped outside, Little Brother said, "I'm so thirsty. If only I could find a stream so I could have a drink."

The children's stepmother was actually a witch. She had followed the children from the moment they left home. She was so angry that the children had escaped. The evil woman was hiding behind a tree when she overheard Little Brother speak. She vowed to teach them a lesson. So she cast a spell on all the streams in the forest.

When Little Brother found the first stream, he bent down to take a drink. "Wait!" Little Sister cried. "The stream is saying something to me. It says, 'Anyone who drinks from me will turn into a tiger.'

"Little Brother," she continued, "please do not drink from here. If you do, you'll turn into a ferocious tiger and tear me to pieces."

"All right," Little Brother said, "I'll wait until we find the next stream."

When they came upon the next stream, Little Sister heard it say, "Anyone who drinks from me will turn into a wolf."

"Little Brother," she cried, "do not drink! If you do, you will turn into a wolf and then you will eat me up."

"Fine," he said, "I will not drink this water, either. But I don't care what the stream says next time. I'm going to take a nice, long drink."

The next stream they found said to Little

Sister, "Anyone who drinks from me will become a fawn, or young deer."

"Wait!" Little Sister shouted. But it was too late. Her brother had already bent over the water. He was taking a nice, long drink.

"Oh no," said Little Sister as she watched Little Brother change into a fawn. They both started to cry. Little Sister said, "Don't worry, Little Brother. I'll take care of you."

She took off her golden necklace and placed it around his neck. Then she braided some long grass to make a leash. She led the fawn deeper into the forest.

They came to an empty cabin in the woods. "This looks like a good place to stay," Little Sister said. "You wait inside. I'll look around for anything to make this place more comfortable."

Little Sister gathered up some leaves and moss to make a soft bed for the fawn. The next morning, and every morning after that, she gathered food for the two of them. During the day, Little Sister and the fawn played together. The fawn would run and run, and Little Sister would chase him. At night, she rested her head on his soft back and fell asleep.

Little Sister spent many years in the forest taking care of her brother, the fawn. She grew into a kind, gentle young woman.

One day, the king of the land decided to hold a great hunt. The forest came alive with sounds of horns, dogs, and the cries of hunters. The fawn longed to be a part of the action. He wanted excitement. He asked his sister to let him go.

Little Sister said, "No! I cannot let you go. What would I do if anything happened to you?"

The fawn promised his sister nothing bad would happen. He knew he was quick enough to outrun the hunters. The fawn begged and begged. Finally, Little Sister opened the door to let him outside.

"You must come home before nightfall. When you are at the door, say to me, 'Little Sister please let me in.' That is how I'll know it's you."

The fawn ran off as fast as he could. The king and his hunters caught sight of him. They chased the fawn, but he was too quick. When it started to get dark, he pranced home. At the front door he said, "Little Sister, please let me in."

She opened the door and he leaped inside. Little Sister was so happy to see the fawn return. Soon the pair were sleeping soundly.

The hunt started all over again the next morning. Again, the fawn begged his sister to let him go. Again, she didn't want him to leave. She told him to be home before dark. "Make sure you say exactly what I told you to say, or else I will not let you in."

The king and his hunters searched for the fawn again. They chased him through the dense woods and even managed to hurt his foot. But the fawn was too fast to be caught. The king ordered one of his hunters to quietly follow the fawn. "Find out how he keeps hiding from us," he said.

The hunter crept silently behind the fawn, and watched as he limped home. He finally came upon the cabin where Little Sister lived with the fawn. The hunter overheard the fawn say, "Little Sister, please let me in."

Little Sister opened the door and gasped when she saw that the fawn was hurt. She washed his cut and soothed it with herbs. By morning, it was all better.

Meanwhile, the hunter went back to find the king's group. He told the king all about the strange fawn, what he said, and where to find the cabin.

The king thought, *tomorrow during the hunt, I'll trick the girl into letting me in. Then I'll surprise the fawn when he comes home. That's how I'll catch him.*

The next day, the hunt began again.

"If I don't go," the fawn said, "I'll die of sadness. The sound of the horns makes me want to move. I need to run. I just have to be myself."

Little Sister sadly opened the door, and the fawn dashed out to meet the hunt. When she closed the door behind him, a tear slid down her cheek.

The king saw the fawn running through the forest. He said to his men, "Hunt him all day and into the night, but don't hurt him. I have a very good plan to catch him." He left his men and went to the fawn's cabin. The king knocked on the cabin door. He said, "Little Sister, please let me in."

When Little Sister opened the door, she was shocked. "You are not the fawn!" she cried.

The king was surprised to see such a beautiful young lady. He fell in love with her on the spot. The king bent his head and asked, "May I come in, beautiful lady?"

Little Sister was also shocked to see a handsome man with a gold crown on his head. She said, "Of course. Please come in."

As the king stepped inside, he was overcome with love for the kind, gentle, and beautiful Little Sister. In the doorway, the king bent down on one knee and asked her, "Would you come to the palace and be my wife?"

Little Sister replied, "Only if my fawn can come, too."

The king smiled kindly. "Of course he may come. He will have anything he needs."

Little Sister could not contain her joy. She and the king spent the day talking and laughing. Little Sister told the king about their awful stepmother. She explained why they had left home and how her Little Brother had turned into a fawn.

As night fell, the fawn leaped into the house. Little Sister found her old grass leash and tied it to the golden necklace the fawn still wore around his neck. She told him that the king wanted to marry her and take care of both of them forever.

The three of them arrived back at the king's castle. A great wedding feast was waiting for them. The royal couple were married that night. They were very happy, and so was the fawn. He had a whole garden and castle grounds to play in.

The news of the king's happy marriage spread across the land. Soon the queen gave birth to a little boy. Everyone in the kingdom celebrated the new prince. Word of the marriage and baby traveled to the evil stepmother.

She was furious to learn that Little Sister and the fawn were happy and well. She was also jealous that Little Sister was now a queen.

"How did they escape my spell? How dare she end up so happy? I must get my revenge!"

The stepmother turned to her ugly, one-eyed daughter and said, "You and I will go to the king's castle. I will cast a spell on the queen to put her in a deep trance. Then we will lock her away. You will take her place as queen and mother. I will charm the king so he doesn't notice the change. The king will no longer have her for his wife, and I will have my revenge. Their happy lives will be ruined forever. And you will become queen!"

The next afternoon, while the king was out, the witch crept into the castle disguised as a maid. The fawn, who usually grazed on the castle's grounds, had gone off with the king. If he had seen his awful stepmother, he would have been able to warn his sister.

The queen was asleep in her room when her wicked stepmother arrived disguised as a maid. The witch cackled as she picked up the queen and carried her away.

Tired and groggy from giving birth, the queen could not fight back. Her stepmother took her to a room in the castle that no one even knew about. Then the evil witch put her into a trance.

"You will sleep here until the end of your days. You will never see your son grow up, and you'll never see your husband again," the witch cackled. She crept silently out of the room— forgetting to lock the door.

She raced back down the castle hallway.

Then she snuck her daughter into the queen's bedroom. She hid the ugly girl's bad eye from view and waited for the king to return.

The great king arrived in his wife's bedroom, eager to see his queen. He was surprised to see a maid he didn't know. The disguised witch said sweetly, "Sire, your wife needs her rest. It's best not to disturb her."

"All she needs is some fresh air and sunshine," the king said, and he got up to open the window. The witch quickly spoke the charm and put him under the spell. It worked! The king didn't notice it was the ugly girl lying in his queen's bed.

"Later," the witch said, "once she's woken from her nap."

The king sighed, but he did just what she wanted. He left the bedroom.

Late that night, at midnight, the real queen crept down to the nursery. She was still in her trance. She opened the nursery door quietly and walked over to the baby's bassinette. The baby's nurse was there. Then she looked out the window at her fawn.

"Your Majesty," the nurse said. "Is everything all right?" But the nurse noticed that something was not right with the queen. She walked strangely. There was an empty look in her eyes. The nurse saw all of this, but she was too afraid to tell the king.

Over the next few nights, the queen came to the nursery at midnight. She walked toward her baby, then looked out the window at the fawn. The nurse had gotten used to the queen's strange walk and odd look. But then the queen spoke. "Where's my child? Where's my fawn? Two more times and then I'm gone."

The nurse was frightened. What did these words mean? The nurse tried to speak to the queen, but she didn't get an answer.

The next night, the queen came in to the nursery again. This time she said, "Where's my child? Where's my fawn? One more time and I'm gone." This time the nurse knew she had to alert the king.

In the morning, the nurse told the king what had been going on in the nursery. "I believe something is *very* wrong with the queen," she said to him.

"Oh my," the king said. "This is strange, indeed. What could be happening with my dear wife? I will spend the night in the nursery and see if I can figure out the problem."

That night, the king watched as the queen did exactly as the nurse had said. Only this time, the queen said, "Where's my child? Where's my fawn? After this, I'm really gone."

"No!" shouted the king. "You are my queen! You must not leave." He gently touched her cheek. That broke the witch's spell.

The queen opened her clear blue eyes. She felt as if she'd been sleeping for a long time. "Oh, my dear husband! You have broken my stepmother's awful curse. She put me into a trance. I was awake on the inside but asleep on the outside. I knew what she was doing but I couldn't stop her. She's pretending to be a maid!"

"Why, I saw that maid in our bedroom. There must also be someone pretending to be you, sleeping in our bed!"

The queen said, "It must be my awful stepsister. Quick! We must catch them before they realize you have broken the spell."

The king sent his soldiers to the bedroom. They burst through the door and saw the evil stepmother and her ugly daughter. The soldiers caught the women. They brought the evil pair to the king and queen.

"You are never to set foot in this kingdom

again!" the king announced. "If you ever show your faces here again, you will be thrown in jail forever."

The king continued, "But first, you will turn Little Brother back into a human."

With one wave of her hand, the witch changed Little Brother back into a human. Then the king's soldiers marched the evil pair to the edge of the kingdom. They left them to wander in the great, vast forest. Nobody ever heard from them again.

Little Brother was so happy he was back to his normal, human form. He hugged Little Sister, who had tears of happiness in her eyes.

Little Brother had grown into a handsome, strong young man. The king placed him in charge of his large army. Even though he wasn't a fawn any longer, he still loved to run. Little Sister, queen again, lived a long and happy life with her king and their son.

CHAPTER 3

Rapunzel

⌒

Once upon a time, there lived a man and his wife who wanted to have a family more than anything. After many years of trying but not having children, they hoped their luck would soon change.

The couple lived next door to a beautiful garden that was owned by a powerful witch. The garden had colorful flower beds where birds would land and sing. There were rows of green leafy vegetables. Thick vines grew up the high walls surrounding the beautiful garden.

One day, the young wife looked out her window at the witch's garden. She saw a beautiful patch of rapunzel, a delicious kind of lettuce. She was so taken with the sight of the fresh, green, tasty lettuce that she simply had to eat some. Weeks went by and all she wanted to eat was this rapunzel. The wife grew thinner and thinner. Rapunzel became the only thing she wanted to eat. Nothing else.

Her husband noticed how pale and thin she looked. He asked, "Dear wife, what is the matter?"

"If I don't eat some of that rapunzel from the old witch's garden, I might go crazy," she replied, hungrier than ever. "It just looks so delicious. I have to have it!"

Of course, the man wanted to give his wife anything she asked for. After sundown, he climbed over the garden wall and pulled some of the rapunzel from the ground. When he returned home, his wife grabbed it from his hands even before saying hello. She made a delicious salad and wolfed the meal down in just three bites.

"From now on, the only food I shall eat is rapunzel," she announced when she finished.

The next day, at sunset, the man grabbed hold of a strong vine. He used it to pull himself over the wall of the garden again. Stepping around some green beans, he arrived at the patch of rapunzel. He broke off many leaves and stuffed them into a little canvas bag. When he finally looked up, he had an awful fright—the old witch stood right before him!

"Thief!" she cried. "How dare you sneak in here and steal my rapunzel? I must punish you."

"Please," the man said, "I simply had to take some of your lettuce. My wife saw it from our window and had to have some. She will not eat anything else. I cannot bear to watch her starve to death."

The witch looked at him closely. "If you are telling the truth, I will give you as much rapunzel as your wife can eat. In return, you must promise to do as I ask." The man agreed. "When the time is right," the witch said, "I will tell you what I want."

Soon the man and his wife learned that she was pregnant. They were overjoyed by their good fortune.

The woman said, "I'm so happy—both by our good news and because I can eat delicious rapunzel every day. I don't even care what you had to promise the old witch—it was worth it!"

The man no longer had to sneak over the wall or fear getting caught. The witch had given him a key to her garden. He picked as much rapunzel as his wife could eat.

A few months later, they had a beautiful, healthy baby girl. In honor of the leaf that kept her alive, the woman named her daughter

Rapunzel. Days after Rapunzel was born, the witch showed up on their doorstep.

"You promised," she said to the man, "to do as I asked. You have taken my rapunzel for months, and now I will take your child."

The woman cried, "No! He never would have made that promise!"

The witch said, "He promised to do exactly as I asked. I want to take this child."

The man knew he could not break his promise. The witch was too powerful. With pain and sadness in his heart, he handed over his baby.

The witch carried her away at once so her parents could never find her. She locked the child in a tall tower with no door and no stairs. Rapunzel was to live there, kept away from the world. There she grew into a beautiful girl.

The witch visited Rapunzel every day. The girl never knew another kind of life. She never met her true parents, and she did not know they missed her very much. The only family she knew was with the old witch, whom she believed was her godmother.

At the top of the tower where Rapunzel lived, there was one tiny window. Whenever the witch wanted to get inside, she stood at the bottom and called out,

Rapunzel, Rapunzel
Let your hair down.

Rapunzel had lovely, long hair the color of fine gold. Whenever she heard the old witch's voice, the girl would fasten her braids to the window's latch. She would let them fall twenty feet to the ground. Then the old witch would grab hold of them and use them to climb up the tower walls.

One day, Rapunzel was singing sweet songs to fill the lonely hours. A young prince happened to be riding through the forest. He became enchanted by Rapunzel's voice. He followed the sound all the way to her tower. When he arrived, all he could see was a girl's shadow in the tiny window at the top.

He climbed down from his horse and looked for a way to meet her. He quickly learned that the tower had no door and no stairs. The more he realized he couldn't get in, the harder he tried. The louder Rapunzel sang her sweet song, the more his heart melted.

There has to be a way up, he thought. *I need to know whose beautiful voice that is. Maybe I could hide and see how she gets in and out . . .*

He hid behind a nearby tree, hoping to find a way to get into the tower. While he crouched there, he saw the old witch come to the tower. He heard her say:

Rapunzel, Rapunzel
Let your hair down.

He watched Rapunzel throw her braids down from the window. Then he saw the witch grab hold of them and climb up the tower wall.

So that's how to get up there! the prince said to himself. *I'm going to try it, too.*

Once the old witch left, the prince stood beneath the tower and called out,

Rapunzel, Rapunzel
Let your hair down.

Long golden braids spilled from the window and dangled in front of him. He climbed up the tower and through the window.

Rapunzel was shocked to see a man in front of her. The only person Rapunzel had ever seen was her godmother. Scared, she screamed and ran into the corner of her room. But the prince spoke so kindly that soon she wasn't afraid.

"Once I heard your beautiful melodies," the prince said, "I knew that you would hold my heart forever. Will you marry me? I want to listen to you sing for the rest of our lives."

Rapunzel didn't know what she should do. How could she leave the tower? Her godmother had forbidden her from ever stepping foot outside it.

"I think I would like to go with you," Rapunzel said shyly, "and see what life is like outside this tower." She placed her little hand in his. In an instant, she knew he would be more loving than her godmother. Her heart warmed to him. "Yes," Rapunzel continued, "I would like to marry you.

"There is no way for both of us to escape the tower, but I have an idea. Every time you come to visit me, bring a small bit of silk rope with you. I will braid a ladder. When it is done, we will climb down it together." The prince promised

he would bring a bit of silk rope with him every time he visited.

"Come in the evening," Rapunzel added. "My godmother always visits during the day."

The prince promised he would see her every single night. He climbed out of her window and left. Rapunzel heard the young prince singing to himself until he was gone from her sight.

Of course, the witch did not know there was a prince visiting Rapunzel. And Rapunzel could think of nothing but her prince. One day, the young girl said by accident, "Godmother, why do you take so long to climb up the tower? When my prince calls, he climbs up my hair so quickly." Rapunzel immediately let out a gasp. She knew she had made an awful mistake.

The witch was furious. "What have you done, you wicked girl?" she screamed. "I locked you in this tower for one reason—to keep you away from the world. That includes princes! There is only trouble and pain in the world. I wanted to save you from this. But you have tricked me. Everything is ruined!"

The old witch grabbed Rapunzel's braid. She pulled a pair of giant scissors from her pocket and cut off all her golden hair. Rapunzel was so shocked, she could not move. Tears fell down her beautiful cheeks.

Then the witch lifted her hands and cast an awful spell on the girl. Rapunzel shrank away and shut her eyes tight. She could not bear to see the anger in her godmother's face. When Rapunzel opened her eyes again, she found herself all alone in the middle of the deep, dark forest. The witch had sent her far, far away.

When the prince came to the tower that evening, he said,

Rapunzel, Rapunzel
Let your hair down.

As usual, the braid fell to the ground. The prince climbed up as he had always done. But once he was inside the tower he didn't find his beloved Rapunzel. Instead the old witch stood in front of him. She was glaring at him.

"You will never see your Rapunzel again," she cackled. "I've sent her deep into the forest where you will never find her." She took a step forward and raised her bony arms. "Now I'm going to punish you, too."

But before the old witch could cast a spell on him, the prince jumped out of the window. He landed on top of a large, thorny bush. The needles scratched his eyes and made him blind. He was miserable and lost. Worst of all, he had no idea where the witch had sent Rapunzel. He wandered through the forest for days, eating only berries and roots. He vowed he would spend forever trying to find her.

Many years passed. The blind prince stumbled through the woods. He had almost given up hope of ever finding his beloved Rapunzel.

But one day, he heard her sweet voice again. For a moment, he thought he was going mad. The prince walked toward the sound. It led him to his beloved Rapunzel. The couple embraced and rejoiced.

Rapunzel saw that the prince's eyes were hurt. "Are you hurt, my love?" When the prince nodded yes, she began to cry. Two of her tears dropped into both of his eyes. The tears must have held magic, for right away they healed the prince's eyes. He could see again!

Rapunzel and her prince found their way through the dark forest back to his kingdom. And there they lived in happiness and good health for many long years.

CHAPTER 4

Hansel and Grethel

∽

Once upon a time, a poor woodcutter lived with his two children and his wife, their stepmother, in a little cottage beside a great forest. The little boy was called Hansel, and his sister's name was Grethel. The family was very poor. One day, the woodcutter could no longer afford even bread.

He sighed and said to his wife, "How will we take care of the children when we have no food to eat?"

The stepmother said, "When the sun comes up tomorrow, we will take them deep into the woods. We will leave them with a warm fire and a stale crust of bread. They will never find their way home. Then we can get on with our lives without them."

"I could never do that!" the woodcutter said. "They will be torn to pieces by wild beasts."

"Foolish man," she said. "We will all just starve then."

The stepmother spoke of nothing else but her plan. Eventually, the woodcutter agreed that it was the only thing they could do. "I will never forgive myself, though. You should know that I will think of them every day," the woodcutter said to his wife.

The family cottage was so small that the children heard every word their parents said. Grethel cried on her brother's shoulder.

Hansel patted his sister on the back and said, "Hush, my dear sister. I have an idea. It will be okay. Try to get some sleep."

Their stepmother woke them up early the next morning. She gave them each a small bit of bread crust. Hansel crushed the bread in his pocket. As they walked deeper and deeper into the forest, he left a tiny trail of bread crumbs.

They finally stopped walking. The family had reached a part of the forest they had never been in before. Hansel and Grethel's stepmother gathered small twigs and leaves and lit a fire. She told the children to take a nap while she and their father gathered some wood. "We will come back to get you when we are done."

The children sat down by the fire. Grethel shared her bread crust with Hansel. Then they fell asleep. When they woke up, it was night. Hansel said to his sister, "We will wait for the moon to shine and then follow my trail of bread crumbs back home."

When the moonlight was bright enough, they tried to find the path home. Hansel and

Grethel looked all around for the bread crumbs. They went farther and farther into the forest.

"The birds must have eaten the bread crumbs I dropped," Hansel said to Grethel.

"Oh no!" she cried. "What should we do now?"

"Don't worry, Grethel," Hansel said. "We will find our way. I know we will."

The children walked day and night for the next three days. Hansel and Grethel grew weary from hunger.

By the afternoon of the third day, the children were too tired and hungry to go on. Ready to give up, they slumped down at the bottom of a very tall tree. Then they heard a sweet white bird singing a pretty song. The children followed her down a path that led to a little house.

When they looked closer at the house, they saw that its walls were made of bread. The roof was made of cake. The windows were made of sparkling sugar. The children were so excited! Hansel stepped forward. "Let's have a taste," he said to his sister. "I'll taste the window, and you can try a piece of the wall."

The children broke off bits of the house to eat. They happily and greedily munched away. Then they heard a voice come from inside,

Nibble, nibble, where's the mouse?
Who's that eating my house?

Hansel replied, "Just two children who are very hungry."

Hansel knocked out an entire sugar windowpane. Grethel tore another large piece of bread from the wall. The children were so busy eating, they didn't notice that the door to the house had opened. A very old, ugly woman stepped outside. She leaned on a crutch, wagged

her finger, and said, "Well, well, dear little children. How in the world did you get here? Come in, come in! No harm will come to you in my house."

The old woman led them inside. She fed them a great meal of apples, pancakes, and nuts. There were two tidy, comfy beds for them to sleep in, too. Soon brother and sister were tucked in and sleeping soundly.

But the old woman was really a wicked witch, only pretending to be kind. She had been walking in the forest when she saw the children slumped down by the tall tree. She had said to herself, *They will be tasty to eat.*

So she charmed a bird and let it guide them back to her house. Before they arrived, she cast a spell that turned her cabin into sweet treats.

Early the next morning, the witch stood by their beds. She thought, *What a tasty meal they will make.*

When Hansel woke up, the old witch grabbed him and locked him in the shed. He cried and cried, but no one could hear him. Grethel then woke up, too. The witch told her, "Get some water to cook your brother some breakfast. He needs to fatten up so I can eat him!"

Grethel began to cry. She was scared of the witch, so she obeyed her demands. She made Hansel a fattening breakfast, and only ate crumbs herself. Each day, the witch would go out to the shed to see how fat Hansel was getting.

"Stick out your finger, Hansel, so I can see how fat you're getting!" the old witch demanded.

Hansel stuck an old bone through the barred door. He knew the witch would eat him when he got fat, so he tried to trick her into thinking he was skinny. It worked! The old witch's eyesight was terrible—she couldn't tell the old bone from Hansel's own finger!

"I'm feeding you and feeding you," the witch

said. "Why don't you grow any fatter? Your fingers are so bony! From now on, you'll be getting even larger portions!" Days passed, and soon the old witch grew tired of waiting.

"Grethel," she called. "Get some water, and be quick about it. I will be cooking and eating Hansel today."

Grethel filled up the kettle and lit the fire. She was shaking so much that she could barely work. Tears streamed down her cheeks, adding to the salty water in the kettle.

The witch said, "First, we need to do the baking. I've already got the dough ready." She pushed Grethel near the oven. "Crawl in and see if the oven is warm enough for the bread."

Grethel said to the witch, "I don't know how to crawl inside. Would you please show me?"

"Silly girl," the witch said, "there's plenty of room." She crawled into the oven and said, "See, I can get right in."

Quickly Grethel slammed the oven door shut and locked it. The old, nasty witch howled and screamed. Grethel ran outside and released Hansel from the shed.

She shouted to him, "Hansel! It's okay. I've put the wicked old witch in the oven. We are now free!"

Hansel said, "Now that there's nothing to fear, let's see what we can take from the old witch's house. Maybe if we go home with riches, our stepmother won't try to leave us in the forest again. Then we will be able to stay with Father. I miss him terribly."

They searched every corner of the house and stuffed their pockets full of gold, pearls, and jewelry. Then they ran away far from the witch's house.

Hansel and Grethel walked for hours trying to find their way home. Finally, they could see their father's house in the distance. Hansel and Grethel ran toward it. They threw open the front door and ran into their father's arms.

"Oh, children," he cried. "I am so happy to see you. I have been looking for you since we left you in the forest. Where have you been?"

Hansel and Grethel explained what had happened in the forest and at the witch's house.

"What a terrible adventure you've had," their father said. The old woodcutter hugged both his children as if he never wanted to let them go.

"Where's our stepmother?" Hansel asked. "She'll be pleased that we've brought such riches home. Here, let us show you!" They pulled the gold, pearls, and jewelry from their pockets.

"You've been gone so long," the father said. "Your stepmother became very sick soon after we left you. She grew weak very quickly. Now she is gone." Hansel and Grethel's father looked sad, so they hugged him again.

Their father continued, "But with all of these riches, we will no longer be poor or hungry."

He was right. The little family lived together in happiness. Never again did they live hungry or apart from one another.

CHAPTER 5

Cinderella

∽

Once upon a time, there lived a rich man whose wife was very ill. Before she passed away, she called for her daughter.

"Cinderella," she said, "be good and do everything you are told. I will look down on you from wherever I am and always be with you."

Cinderella promised her mother that she would be good and obedient. Just days later, Cinderella's mother passed away. The girl was sad beyond belief.

Before long, Cinderella's father remarried. Her new stepmother brought two daughters to live with them. The two girls were very pretty on the outside. But they were mean and nasty on the inside. Cinderella's stepmother and stepsisters made her life hard whenever her father was not there. When he was around, they pretended to be kind to Cinderella. Her father never knew how cruel they really were. Cinderella never told him.

From morning until night, Cinderella worked very hard. She carried water, got the fire going, cooked, cleaned, and washed. The girl never had a moment's rest. Her evil stepmother and stepsisters wouldn't even let her sleep in her own bed at night. Instead, they made her lie down near the fire. And so she was always covered in dust and ash. The sisters cackled and said, "No wonder she's called Cinderella."

One day, their father was going in to town. He asked all the girls what he could bring back for them.

"Dresses and pearls for every one of us," the stepsisters said.

"Father," Cinderella said, "please break off the first branch that brushes against your hat on the way home."

"That's a strange request. Are you sure you wouldn't like dresses and pearls like your stepsisters?" her father asked.

"I'd like to plant it in the garden, near my mother's grave."

Her father patted her on the shoulder and said, "Then I shall find you a lovely branch that will grow into a beautiful tree."

When their father came back home, he had beautiful jewels and dresses for the stepsisters. He handed a small hazel branch to Cinderella. That afternoon, she planted the small sprout right next to where her mother was laid to rest. Cinderella hoped something beautiful would grow to honor her mother.

The next few months were awful for Cinderella. Her stepmother and stepsisters were nasty to her. For comfort, she visited her mother's grave. She cried and cried beside the little hazel branch. Her tears watered it so much that it quickly grew into a tall tree. Soon a little white bird came to live in the tall hazel tree. Anytime Cinderella made a wish, the little bird happily fulfilled it.

One day, the king announced he would hold a festival to find his son a bride. The whole kingdom was to attend. Cinderella's family received an invitation, but she knew her stepmother would never let her go.

The evening of the festival arrived. The stepsisters made Cinderella comb their hair and help them get dressed in beautiful silk gowns.

Cinderella begged her stepmother to let her go, too.

"Cinderella," she said, "how can you possibly go anywhere? You have no shoes or dress, and you are covered in dirt."

"But what if my father asks why I'm not going with you? Surely he wants me to go."

Her stepmother answered, "I've told him you are ill."

Then the stepmother hurried into the carriage with her two daughters. They raced away to the ball before Cinderella could say another word.

Cinderella went outside to the back garden to cry. She sat under her hazel tree by her mother's grave and said,

Shake your branches, little tree.
Toss gold and silver down to me.

The little white bird granted her wishes. A dress of gold and silver, and beautiful silk slippers fell from the sky.

"Thank you!" Cinderella cried. "This is the loveliest dress I've ever seen." She slipped it on and raced toward the palace to attend the festival.

When Cinderella arrived, the ballroom was lit by candles and filled with people. Music echoed throughout the halls. Couples were laughing and dancing. All was joyful and merry. But everyone stopped and stared the moment Cinderella entered the room.

Her dress was elegant, and she looked radiant. Many of the king's guests thought she must be the daughter of a visiting king. Even her father, stepmother, and stepsisters didn't recognize her!

The prince noticed her immediately. He stepped forward to welcome her to the ball.

"Would you like to dance with me?" he asked kindly. She smiled and said, "Yes." He took her hand and led her to the dance floor. They danced together all night.

The prince was enchanted by her. Whenever another woman would approach him to dance, he would simply say, "No, thank you. I already have a dance partner."

It grew very late. Cinderella told the prince that she had to go home. He offered to take her there, but she refused. When the prince turned around for a moment, Cinderella slipped away.

Where could she have gone? the prince thought. *I cannot believe I've lost sight of her. I must find her.*

He spent the rest of the evening looking for Cinderella. And he still refused to dance with anyone else.

By the time Cinderella's family arrived back home, she was dressed in her rags, asleep by the kitchen fire. She looked as dirty as ever.

On the final day of the festival, Cinderella
went back to the tree at her mother's grave. She
called out as she had before,

Shake your branches, little tree.
Toss gold and silver down to me.

Another fine dress fell down to her, and this
time she also received slippers covered in gold.
She hurried off to the ball.

The prince grinned ear-to-ear when he saw
her come into the ballroom—he could not take
his eyes off her. No one else existed for him.

"I'm so glad you came tonight," he said. "I
just wish you would not disappear again." He
winked at her. Cinderella smiled as he led her
onto the dance floor.

"I'm going to be careful not to let you out
of my sight," the prince said. Cinderella worried
for a moment that she wouldn't be able to get

home. What if her stepmother and stepsisters found out she had been coming to the ball?

I'll have to slip away, she thought. *I'll do it the first moment he's not looking.*

For a little while, Cinderella let herself get carried away by the party. The prince was so kind, and he danced so well. She had never felt happier.

There was a break in the music, and the prince led Cinderella off the dance floor. The pair stood in the doorway of the castle, admiring the night sky. The king came out to speak with the prince. The moment the prince turned to greet him, Cinderella slipped away.

But the clever prince had figured Cinderella might try to escape again. He had his servants cover the staircase in sticky tar—anyone trying to race down the stairs would stick. Cinderella did get stuck, but she managed to free her foot from its golden slipper. She fled the palace.

It all happened so fast. The prince suddenly noticed Cinderella had slipped away. He ran outside hoping to catch her. All he found was her golden slipper stuck on the stairs. Breathless, he reached down to pick it up.

Cinderella raced home, quickly changed, and lay down in her usual place. Just moments later everyone arrived back home.

The next morning, the prince brought the shoe to his father. "The woman whose foot fits this golden shoe will be my bride," he said. "I must find her!"

The prince and his footmen visited every house in the land. The tiny, delicate shoe didn't fit a single girl—no one had feet so small.

The very last house he visited was Cinderella's. When the stepsisters learned the reason for the prince's visit, they became very excited. They both thought they had beautiful, small feet. Each girl was sure the slipper would fit her!

The eldest sister went into her bedroom to try it on. She couldn't get her big toe to fit in the shoe. Her mother said, "Oh, bend your toe all the way. It may hurt now, but once you are queen you will not need to walk."

The girl forced her foot into the shoe. She swallowed her pain and went out to meet the prince. Once he saw the shoe fit, he immediately took her for his bride. They left on horseback. As they rode past the hazel tree by the grave, the little white bird called out,

The foot's too long and far too wide!
Go back and find the proper bride.

The prince looked down and saw how poorly the shoe fit. He turned around and took the stepsister right back to the house.

Then it was the younger sister's turn to try on the gold slipper. Of course, it was too small. Her mother said, "Force your heel in, my girl! What will blisters matter when you are queen?"

The girl limped out to meet the prince, who was delighted to see that the shoe fit her. He lifted her up onto his horse to take her back to the castle. When they passed by the hazel tree, the bird called out again,

The foot's too long and far too wide!
Go back and find the proper bride.

The prince noticed that the stepsister's heel was red and raw. She could barely keep the shoe on her foot. The prince swiftly turned his horse around. Once back at the house, he said to Cinderella's father, "Do you have another daughter?"

The father replied, "There's no one left but Cinderella, the daughter of my first wife. She cannot possibly be who you are looking for. She was too ill to attend the ball."

"Send for her immediately," the prince said. "I have vowed to see every single girl in the land. She is the only one left."

Cinderella's heart leaped when she heard this. She scrubbed her hands and face until there was not a spot of dirt to be found. Then she went out to meet the prince.

Cinderella curtsied before him, and he handed her the golden slipper. She sat down on a stool and slipped it on. It fit perfectly! When she stood up, the prince remembered her elegance and her sweet, beautiful face. He shouted, happily, "You are the girl from the ball. You are my beautiful mystery woman!"

The prince got down on one knee and asked her to marry him. Cinderella said "Yes" and embraced her dear prince.

The prince picked up Cinderella and carried

her out of the house. He set her upon his horse and climbed up.

"To the castle!" the prince shouted, and kissed his bride. As they rode through the back garden, the little white bird from the hazel tree sang,

The foot's not too long, nor too wide.
The true bride's riding at his side.

Cinderella and her prince lived happily ever after.

CHAPTER 6

Briar Rose

◦~

Long, long ago, there lived a king and queen who wanted to have a child more than anything else. One sunny day, the queen was sitting by a stream. A frog jumped out of the water and said, "Your wish will be granted. Before this year is over, you'll have a daughter."

The queen was surprised. *How strange!* she thought as she walked home.

"Maybe it will come true," the king said when he heard the story. "Stranger things have happened."

They laughed and thought no more of it. But then one day the queen became pregnant. The royal couple was overjoyed! The queen gave birth to a little girl—the frog's words came true. When the king saw his beautiful daughter for the first time, he was so happy. He ordered there be a great feast in the kingdom to celebrate.

The king thought about whom he should invite. Among his subjects were the thirteen Wise Women. These fairies were famous for granting wishes. The king wanted to make sure they would always be kind to his daughter. However, there was one problem: The king had only twelve golden plates. One of the Wise Women would have to stay behind. The king invited his friends, family, and twelve Wise Women. Soon the feast day arrived.

All day the king entertained his guests with delightful music and wonderful food. People marveled at the happy, healthy baby they called

Rose. When the evening was coming to an end, the twelve Wise Women offered their magic gifts to the princess.

The first Wise Woman twirled over to the cradle and gave the princess goodness. The second one gave her eternal beauty. The third Wise Woman gave her wealth. This continued until eleven of the Wise Women had given their gifts. The girl already had everything anyone could ever want.

Then the twelfth Wise Woman stood up to give her gift to the baby. But before she approached the cradle, the thirteenth Wise Woman—the one who was not invited—arrived in a cloud of smoke and fire. She was a very angry fairy, and could not believe she had not been invited to the feast. This Wise Woman had a wicked gift. "When this child turns fifteen," she told the king and queen, "she will prick her finger on a spindle and fall down dead."

The moment she finished the curse, the fairy disappeared. The entire dining hall fell silent. The king and queen shook with fear and horror.

The queen turned to the king with shock in her eyes. "What shall we do?"

The king called out to the twelfth Wise Woman, "You have not yet given your gift, Wise Woman. What chance do we have that you can save our beloved Rose?"

She answered, "Sadly, our magic cannot be reversed. But I can alter the curse. When the princess pricks her finger at age fifteen, she will not die. Instead, she will fall into a deep sleep that will last for one hundred years."

The morning after the feast, the king ordered all of the spindles in the kingdom to be destroyed. He said to his wife, "If there are no spindles, there is no way our darling Rose will prick her finger."

As the years passed, all of the Wise Women's

gifts came to be for the young princess. She grew up to be good, beautiful, bright, and charming.

On the morning of her fifteenth birthday, the king and queen would not let Princess Rose out of their sight. As the family sat down for a birthday lunch, a servant ran into the dining hall. Almost out of breath, he told the king there was an emergency. Only the king and queen could attend to the problem. They fled from the dining hall to handle to their royal duties.

The princess was left all alone. She roamed around the castle, poking her head into room after room. There were many places in the castle where Princess Rose was normally not allowed to go.

She came upon a stairwell that led to an old tower. "What is this?" Rose said. Curiosity pulled her up the stairs. She found an old door with a rusty key in the lock. The princess turned the key, opened the door, and stepped into a tiny room. An old woman was sitting there, spinning wool at a spindle.

"Good afternoon," the princess said. "What are you doing?"

The old woman replied, "I'm spinning wool."

Rose watched the strange machine dip up and down. She became even more curious.

"What is this?" she asked as she reached forward to touch the needle. Before the princess could say another word, she pricked her finger on the spindle.

Immediately the princess fell to the floor, and a deep sleep came over her. The spell spread throughout the castle, putting everyone to sleep. Even the king and queen, who had just returned, fell to the floor instantly. The horses fell asleep in their stables. The dogs fell asleep in the courtyard. Even the wind stopped blowing. The twelfth Wise Woman's words had come true.

Many years passed. The castle and everything

inside it slept. A thorny briar bush grew thick and tall around the castle. Every year it grew taller. Over time, it grew so tall and thick that it was impossible to see even the flags on the castle's towers. Stories spread across the land about the beautiful Briar Rose—trapped asleep in the castle. Year after year, princes would come from far away and try to force their way through the thick briar bush. None could ever make it through.

One day, another young, brave prince heard the story of Briar Rose. "I'm going to find the castle and free the princess!" he exclaimed.

The prince finally arrived after months of searching. But he did not find a giant briar bush there as other princes had. Instead, he found a path of beautiful flowers leading his way to the castle. Inside the courtyard, he found the sleeping dogs and the sleeping horses. He found a sleeping cook fallen over his hundred-year-old stew. Even the flies were not moving. The king and queen were asleep next to their thrones.

The prince searched every room in the castle—the ballroom, the dining room, the kitchen, the bedrooms. He made his way down hallway after quiet hallway. The very disappointed prince was about to give up on ever finding Briar Rose.

I'll take one last look, he thought to himself, *and then I must go.*

He kicked open an old door that led to a dusty hallway. At the end, he found the staircase that led to the tower. The prince slowly climbed up the dark stairs. The rusty key was still in the lock. He opened the door.

A girl lay on the floor. It had to be Briar Rose! The girl was so beautiful that he could not look away from her. He lifted her up and cradled her in his arms. Before he could stop himself, he bent down and kissed her, very gently, on the cheek. His warm heart and kind thoughts immediately broke the sleeping spell.

Briar Rose suddenly woke up, opened her eyes, and smiled at him. Without a word, he took her hand and led her down the stairs of the tower. As they walked through the castle, everything and everyone began to wake up.

Doves freed their heads from underneath their wings. The horses shook themselves awake. The dogs wagged their tails, slowly at first. Rose saw her parents, the king and queen, rubbing the sleep from their eyes. She threw her arms around them.

"This is the prince who woke me from the slumber," she said to the king and queen.

"Lovely to meet you, Your Highnesses." He bowed to them. "If I may, I would like to marry your daughter." The king and queen approved at once.

The two couples walked through the castle, each arm in arm. They passed by the kitchen, and the fire started up again. The royal cook woke up. He began to make a delicious stew. For now he had to prepare for a great feast. The king would soon call for a great celebration to honor the marriage of this young, brave prince to the lovely Briar Rose.

CHAPTER 7

Snow White

~∽~

In the middle of winter, as giant snowflakes blew all around, a pretty queen sat sewing by the window. The queen looked down at the sparkling snow and wished, *If only I had a child with skin as white as snow, hair as black as the wood of this window frame, and lips as red as blood.*

Not long after the queen made her wish, she had a little daughter who looked just as she wanted. The queen named her Snow White. Sadly, the queen died shortly after her daughter was born. A year later, the king remarried a proud, beautiful woman. She didn't like the thought of anyone in the kingdom being more beautiful than she was. Whenever she stood in front of the magic mirror she owned, she would say,

Mirror, mirror, on the wall
Who's the fairest of them all?

The mirror always said the same thing: "You, Queen, are the fairest of them all."

With each passing day, Snow White grew prettier. The new queen was very jealous of the girl's growing beauty. She did everything possible to make the girl appear ugly. This did not bother Snow White, who was good and kind and friendly.

One day, when Snow White was a teenager, the queen asked the mirror who was the fairest one of all. For the first time, it replied, "My Queen, you may be the fairest here. But Snow White is the fairest in all the land."

When the queen heard this, she grew jealous and angry. That afternoon, she called for the kingdom's best hunter. She said to him, "Take Snow White out into the forest. Make sure I never see her again. Before you come back, you'd better have proof that she will never return."

The hunter obeyed the queen's wish and took Snow White deep into the forest. He knew what he had to do. But the girl was so beautiful and charming that he took pity on her. He said, "Hurry up and run away, you poor child. I'll figure out what to tell the queen." Snow White promised to run far away and never return.

Snow White had never been more frightened. For the first time in her life, she was all alone in the forest. She raced over jagged rocks and through sharp thorn bushes. Wild animals stood still and watched as she ran past. Just before the sun disappeared completely, Snow White thought, *Where will I sleep? What will I eat?*

At that moment, she saw a little cottage. Snow White came closer. The small house looked inviting and safe. She tried the front door. It was unlocked. Stepping inside, Snow White noticed everything was tiny. In the dining room was a spotless table set with seven tiny cups, plates, knives, and forks all ready for dinner. There was not a spot of dirt anywhere. Everything was in its correct place—even the seven tiny beds were perfectly made.

Snow White was hungry and thirsty. She took a small bite from each plate and a small sip from each cup on the dining table. She took one look at the seven tiny beds. She was very tired, so she lay down. Soon, Snow White was fast asleep.

The people who lived in the cottage returned after dark. They were seven dwarfs. They worked in the mountains as miners of minerals. Once they went inside their cottage, they lit their seven lanterns and sat down to eat dinner. But they noticed something was strange. Someone had been in their house. The dwarfs began to look around.

They were shocked to find the beautiful young Snow White sleeping in one of their beds. She looked so peaceful that the dwarfs didn't want to wake her up.

In the morning, Snow White opened her eyes. She saw seven dwarfs staring at her. At first she was scared. But then they asked kindly, "What's your name?"

"Snow White," she answered.

"What are you doing in our house?" they wondered.

Snow White told them about her wicked stepmother and how the hunter had saved her life. The dwarfs could see she was frightened, so they were kind to her. They patted her back and said, "You can stay with us as long as you help us around the house."

"Oh yes, of course," Snow White said. "Thank you so much. I can tell you are very nice little gentlemen. We will have a lovely time getting to know one another."

Since Snow White was by herself every day, the dwarfs warned her not to let anyone in the house. They had a feeling that her wicked stepmother would come looking for her.

The next day, the queen asked her magic mirror if she was now the fairest one of all. Of course she thought that Snow White was gone forever. The mirror said,

You're the fairest here, dear Queen.
But little Snow White, far away,
With the seven dwarfs she stays,
Remains the fairest ever seen!

The queen grew angry. The hunter had lied! Snow White was alive and was still the fairest one in the land. Now the queen had to think of another way to get rid of her. She dressed herself up as an old woman and found the dwarfs' cottage in the woods.

"Hello?" the wicked queen called out at the front door of the cottage. "I have many nice, pretty things for sale."

Snow White looked out the window and saw that it was just a harmless old woman. She let her into the cottage. The wicked queen asked Snow White if she wanted to try on a pretty lace top. She helped Snow White put it on. When the wicked queen pulled the strings to lace it up the back, she tied them too tight. So tight, in fact, that Snow White couldn't breathe. She dropped to the floor instantly. *There*, thought the evil queen. *Now I'm the fairest in the land!*

When the seven dwarfs came home after work, they found Snow White on the floor. They noticed that she wasn't breathing and pulled her free from the lacing. Little by little, she came back to life. Snow White told them what had happened to her that afternoon.

They said, "That old woman was your wicked stepmother in disguise! Don't let anyone in unless we are at home."

That night, when she got home, the queen went right to her mirror and asked,

Mirror, mirror on the wall
Who's the fairest of them all?

The mirror replied,

You're the fairest here, dear Queen.
But little Show White, far away,
With the seven dwarfs she stays,
Remains the fairest ever seen!

The queen was outraged! She hid in a secret part of the castle and spent hours creating a magical apple. The apple looked perfect on the outside—crispy and red. But if anyone took even one bite, that person would die. The queen put the apple away in a basket and turned herself into a poor peasant woman to fool Snow White. Then she set off again to the home of the dwarfs.

Snow White heard the knock at the door. She popped her head out the window and said, "I'm not allowed to let anyone in."

The woman said, "I want to give away my delicious apples. Here, let me give you one."

"That's very kind, but no," Snow White said. "I'm not supposed to take anything from strangers."

"It's my best apple," the woman said. She held the shiny, delicious red apple up to the window. Snow White could not take her eyes away. The apple's spell made it impossible to say no. Without even realizing how dangerous it was, Snow White put her hand out and grabbed the fruit. All she did was take one small bite and she fell down as if she were dead.

The witch cackled. She said, "Skin as white as snow, lips as red as blood, hair the color of dark wood. This time, those dwarfs will not be able to bring you back to life!"

That night, she asked the mirror, again, who was the fairest in the land. It replied,

Oh Queen, you are the fairest in the land!

When the dwarfs returned from work, they found Snow White lying on the floor. They unlaced the ties of her shirt, just in case. But it was no use—the poor girl was dead. They wept and wept.

The dwarfs missed their friend so much. She looked so beautiful, even in death, that they could not bring themselves to bury her. Her cheeks were still rosy and red. She even looked like she was still alive. Instead they made a glass coffin so they could always look at her. They wrote her name in gold on the side. On a sign, they described her as the daughter of a king. The dwarfs took the coffin up to the top of a mountain and placed it in a lovely wooded area. They took turns staying there so Snow White would never be alone. Once a week, the dwarfs would all gather beside the coffin to spend time together with Snow White.

Snow White lay in her glass coffin for years. One day, a prince was traveling through the mountains. He came upon the glass coffin that held the beautiful girl. He could not believe how lovely she was with her black hair, red lips, and white skin. He saw the dwarfs gathered around her. He asked why this beautiful girl was lying here in the glass coffin. They told him the story of Snow White. The prince's heart ached for the poor girl.

"Let me take the coffin," he said to the dwarfs. "I will give you whatever you want for it."

The dwarfs replied, "We wouldn't sell it for all the gold in the world."

"I cannot live without being able to see this beautiful girl. Please, I will love and cherish her as if she were my beloved."

The dwarfs saw that the prince was a good and honest man, so they agreed. The prince ordered some of his men to carry the coffin back to his castle. On the way down the mountain, the men stumbled over some rocks. This bump freed the piece of apple from Snow White's throat. The beautiful girl suddenly came back to life!

She knocked on the glass case and waited patiently for the prince to open it. She sat up and said, "Good heavens, where am I? How did I get here? Where are the kind seven dwarfs?"

The prince was shocked. "Your friends, the

seven dwarfs, thought you were dead. They put you in this glass coffin on a mountaintop and guarded it with their lives. I was carrying you down from this mountain because I am in love with you. I decided I must be with you always," he explained to her. The prince was so happy Snow White was awake. He helped her out of the glass coffin. They walked together the rest of the way down the mountain.

The prince took Snow White back to the home of the dwarfs. They, too, were excited and happy to see her alive and safe.

The prince said to Snow White, "You must come and stay with me. I love you more than anything on earth. Please marry me. It would make me the happiest man on earth."

Snow White happily agreed to marry him. He promised the dwarfs he would always keep her safe from harm. They lived together happily ever after, far, far away from the wicked queen.

CHAPTER 8

Rumpelstiltskin

One day, a poor miller was called before the king. He said, "I have a beautiful daughter who can spin straw into gold." This was not the truth. The miller was just trying to impress the king.

"What a useful talent to have!" the king said. "Bring your daughter to the palace tomorrow."

The next day the king took the miller's daughter to a room filled with straw, a spinning wheel, and a spindle. Before he locked the door, he said, "Get to work. If you haven't spun this straw into gold by tomorrow morning, I'll lock you up in the castle prison."

The miller's daughter burst into tears. "What am I going to do?" she said. "I don't know how to spin straw into gold."

Just then, a gnome appeared. "Little girl, why are you crying?"

The girl told him what her father said and what the king had ordered. "Is that all?" the gnome said. "What will you give me to spin this straw into gold for you?"

She thought for a moment, "My necklace?"

"Very well." The gnome sat down and quickly spun all of the straw into gold. Then he disappeared.

The next morning, the king unlocked the door and saw all the gold. His greedy eyes widened. There was a lot of gold. But he knew a king could always use more gold. He took the miller's daughter to a bigger room filled with even more straw: "You have until morning to spin this straw into gold, or else."

The girl was frightened and started to cry. The gnome appeared again. "What will you give me to spin this straw into gold?"

The miller's daughter said, "This ring on my finger."

"Very well," the gnome said. He sat down to spin the straw into gold.

The next morning, the king was happy to see all the gold. But it was still not enough. He took the miller's daughter to an even *bigger* room filled with even *more* straw. "If you spin all of this straw into gold, I will make you my queen. But if you don't, I will lock you away forever."

When the king had gone, the gnome appeared. "What will you give me to turn this straw into gold?" he asked.

The miller's daughter replied, "I have nothing left to give."

"If you promise to give me your firstborn child once you become queen, I will spin all of this straw into gold for you," the gnome said.

Who knows what will happen between now and then, the miller's daughter thought. *No one would actually make a mother give away her child.* So she agreed, desperate to have the gold to please the king. The gnome spun the straw into gold.

The next morning, the king discovered yet another room filled with golden thread. He was so pleased that he arranged the wedding ceremony and feast for that very day.

A year later, the new queen had a healthy, happy baby. She had forgotten all about her promise to the gnome. When he suddenly appeared, asking her to keep her promise, she became very upset.

"I can give you all the treasures in the world. But please let me keep my child," the queen begged him.

"All the treasures in the world were not what you promised me. They are not what I want."

She started to cry, and the gnome felt pity for her. He said, "If you can guess my name, I will let you keep your baby. I will give you three days to do so."

All night long the queen made list upon list of names. She asked all around the kingdom for names that she might have forgotten.

The gnome arrived the next day wanting to hear the queen tell him his name. She started reciting names: Casper, Melchior, Balthasar . . . After she had said every name on her list, the gnome said, "No. You have not said my name. I will be back tomorrow."

The queen asked even more people for new names for her list. When the gnome came to see her the next day, she asked if he was Ribfiend, Muttonchops, or Spindleshanks. She tried the most unusual names she could think of, but each time he said, "No, that is not my name. I will be back tomorrow."

The queen sent messengers to every single corner of the kingdom. She *had* to figure out the little gnome's name! One of the messengers returned on the third day with some news. He said, "I came around a bend in the forest and saw a funny little hut. In it, there was an odd little man dancing around a fire. He said a little rhyme that went,

> *Tomorrow I brew, today I bake*
> *Soon the child is mine to take.*
> *Oh what luck to win this game.*
> *Rumpelstiltskin is my name!*

"Oh, thank you!" she said to the messenger, and gave him a handsome reward.

When the gnome appeared, she asked him, "Is your name Conrad?"

"No, that's not my name," he said. A sly smile crept across his face.

"What about Harry?"

"No."

"Could it possibly be . . . Rumpelstiltskin?"

The little gnome was shocked! "How did you find out?" he shouted. "How did you know?" He stomped his little foot and shook his little fists. But the queen had won the game. Rumpelstiltskin left the palace, never to return.

CHAPTER 9

The Golden Goose

ᏣᏍ

Once there lived a man who had three sons. The youngest was called Simple Simon. The family was ashamed of him because he wasn't very bright. One day, the eldest son went, with a packed lunch, into the forest to chop wood. When he got there, he met a little old gray man.

"Good day," the old man said to the eldest son. "I am very hungry and thirsty. Would you mind sharing your lunch with me?"

The son said, "I have a lot of hard work ahead

of me. If I share my lunch with you, there will not be any left for me."

He walked away and left the little old gray man standing on the path. Later, when the son started to chop the wood, his ax missed the tree and badly cut his arm. The little old gray man had made this happen.

The next day, the middle son decided *he* would go into the forest to chop some wood. His mother packed him a tasty meal. He, too, met the little old gray man. The old man asked if the middle son would share his food and drink with him. The young man said, "I have a very long, hard day of chopping down trees ahead of me. Whatever I give you, I will not have for myself." Once more, the little old gray man was left standing by himself on the path. And once more, he caused some trouble. The middle son struck himself in the leg with the ax and hurt himself.

Simple Simon, the youngest son, said to his father, "Let me go to the forest for the wood while my brothers recover."

"No, you'd better leave it alone, or you'll get hurt, too. You don't know the first thing about using an ax."

But Simple Simon begged his father to let him go, and the man finally agreed. Simple Simon's mother packed him a lunch, too. But she thought he'd be coming home even before lunchtime. When he got to the forest, Simple Simon met the little old gray man. Again, the man said, "Will you share your food with me? I am so hungry and so very thirsty."

"All I have is leftovers," Simple Simon replied. "But I'm happy to share it with you."

The two of them sat down in a pretty meadow. When Simple Simon opened up his basket, he found a delicious meal of tasty pancakes and lemonade. The little old gray man said, "You have such a good heart and were so kind to me. I'm going to grant you good fortune. See that old tree there?" Simple Simon nodded. "If you chop it down, you will find a special treasure at its roots."

Then the little old gray man disappeared. Simple Simon did as he was told. He chopped down the tree and discovered a goose with feathers of pure gold. Simple Simon picked up the golden goose and started walking through the forest. He thought, *I can make my way in the world with this golden goose!* Simple Simon had always wanted to spend a night in an inn, so that's where he headed first.

When Simple Simon arrived at the inn, he met the innkeeper, who introduced him to his three daughters. When the girls saw the glistening, golden feathers of the goose, each wanted to pluck one. He managed to shield the goose and escape to his room.

The moment Simple Simon left his room for dinner, the oldest daughter crept into his room. She tried to pull out one of the golden goose's feathers. But as soon as she touched it, her fingers stuck to the goose. She couldn't pull her hand away. The second sister came in and tried to free her older sister from the golden goose. But the second girl became stuck to her sister! The third sister heard shouting coming from the room. As soon as she arrived, her sisters shouted, "Stay away or else you'll get stuck, too!"

"What are you talking about?" she said and walked over to touch her sister. She, too, became stuck.

Simple Simon returned to his room after dinner. He didn't even notice the girls were stuck to his goose. He fell right into bed and slept until the next morning. He woke up, yawned, threw back the covers, and picked up his goose. He still didn't notice the three girls who were stuck to the golden bird.

He left the inn and took off for the road. The girls had to run behind him, for he walked very fast. They passed a man in a meadow. The poor fellow could not believe his eyes when he saw Simple Simon, the goose, and the three girls go past. He shouted, "What are you girls doing chasing after that silly boy and a goose?" The man went closer to pull the youngest girl away. Well, he got stuck, too!

The entire group carried on. They passed a blacksmith. "Hey, you're blocking the whole street," he shouted at them. "No one can get by!" He chased the chain of people, grabbed the man who was last in line, and ended up stuck, too.

Soon Simple Simon had collected a pastor, a reverend, and one farmer in addition to the blacksmith, the man in the meadow, and the innkeeper's three daughters. It wasn't until the very last person got stuck that he looked behind him. Confused, he said, "What are all you people doing hanging on to my golden goose?"

They sighed and explained that they could not unstick themselves.

"Well," Simple Simon said, "we will just have to carry on like this until we can find a solution."

Later that day, the entire group came into a city. The city was ruled by a king who had a very unhappy daughter. He had said that anyone who could make his girl laugh would be allowed to marry her. Simple Simon heard about this challenge. He decided to bring his entire ridiculous group through the city and see if the princess would laugh.

When the princess saw the young man with the golden goose, three girls, one man, one blacksmith, one pastor, one reverend, and one farmer stuck to it, she started to giggle. Soon she was laughing very hard. Simple Simon was pleased that he would now be able to marry the beautiful princess, who was now happy.

"Here," he said to the king, "let me give you my golden goose to thank you for the honor."

The king ordered his servants to take the group into the castle and get them unstuck.

Meanwhile, the king wasn't sure that Simple Simon would make a good son-in-law. He gave the lad a challenge. "If you can find a man who can drink an entire barrel of water, you can marry my daughter," he told the young man.

Simple Simon suddenly remembered how thirsty the little old gray man was. He went back to the forest to find him.

"Are you still thirsty?" Simple Simon asked the little old gray man.

"I have a huge thirst that I just cannot seem to quench. I am so thirsty," the little old gray man answered.

"Come with me," Simple Simon said. "I know where there's an entire barrel of water you can drink!"

Simple Simon took the little old gray man to the king's palace tower, where he drank until his sides ached. Once again, Simple Simon presented his success to the king.

"May I now marry your daughter?" he asked.

The king gave him a second challenge. "If you can find a man who can eat a mountain full of bread, I'll let you marry my daughter."

The little old gray man was still in the palace tower. Simple Simon went up there to ask him if all that water had made him hungry. The little old gray man said he was starving now that he had had enough to drink. Simple Simon led him to the castle's kitchen, where the cook had prepared an entire mountain of bread. Before the day was done, the little old gray man had eaten every single piece. Simple Simon congratulated him and sent him on his way back home to the forest.

Now, for the third time, Simple Simon stood before the king asking for his daughter's hand in marriage. The king gave him an impossible challenge. "The moment you show me a ship that can sail on both land and water, I'll let you marry my daughter."

This time, Simple Simon had no idea what to do. He knew it was an impossible task. As he walked the lonely path back home through the forest, he came upon his friend, the little old gray man.

"What's wrong?" the old man asked.

Simple Simon replied, "The king's given me an impossible task. He will not let me marry his daughter until I show him a boat that sails both on land *and* on water. I've given up and now I'm going home."

The little old gray man smiled and said, "Simple Simon, you were so kind to me. You gave me enough water to drink and enough bread to eat. You shared your lunch with me when you had so little. Look over there."

Simple Simon looked to where the little old gray man was pointing. There, right in front of his eyes, was a ship that could sail on both land and sea. As Simple Simon rode it all the way to the king's castle, he knew he had finally met all of his challenges. The king allowed the couple to marry that night, and they lived happily for many years.

CHAPTER 10

The Worn-Out Dancing Shoes

◦◦◦

Once upon a time, there lived a king who had twelve daughters. They all slept in one large room with twelve beds side by side. The king didn't want his daughters to get into any kind of trouble. He would lock the door to their bedroom at night. But every morning, when the king came to say good morning to his daughters, he would notice that their shoes were damaged. He held them up to his eyes and inspected them closely. The heels were worn and the toes were scuffed.

The king thought, *Why, heels get worn down from stomping and toes are scuffed by tapping—these girls have been dancing!*

The king could never find out where or how his daughters did all this dancing. He told his kingdom that anyone who learned the truth could choose any of his daughters to marry. That person would also eventually become king. The king said he would give each person three nights to find the answer. If that person didn't succeed, he would have to leave the kingdom forever.

Many princes from many faraway lands came to the castle to try the king's challenge. Strangely, not one of them could stay awake after dinner long enough to discover the truth about the princesses.

A lone soldier was wandering home one night and had to pass through the king's city. He came across an old woman. She told him about the king's challenge and asked him where he was going.

"I don't really know," he answered. "I wouldn't mind trying to find out how the king's daughters wear out their shoes. Then I could become king one day."

The old woman told him about all of the princes who had tried before. How they all fell asleep and failed their tasks. She said, "I have an idea. Try not to eat anything. All of the princes who tried to solve the mystery fell asleep too early." Then she handed him a magic cloak and said, "Pretend you are asleep, then use this to become invisible. You'll have no trouble following the princesses at night."

He folded up the cloak and tucked it away in his bag. Then he approached the king's castle. The king gave him the same chance he had given all of the princes. He led the soldier to the room beside the princesses' room and said, "Someone will be up with your dinner very soon."

When a princess arrived with the food, the soldier pretended to eat it. But he threw it all out the window when she wasn't looking. Then he lay down on the bed and pretended to snore loudly. The princesses saw him fast asleep in his bed. They laughed and ran next door to their room. "Here's another one who'll be sent away forever!" The princesses opened up their closets and pulled out their shimmering dresses. They tied pretty ribbons around their waists and pulled out their shoes. They could hardly wait to start dancing!

The youngest sister said, "I'm worried. I have a feeling this soldier is different. Maybe we shouldn't go tonight?"

Her oldest sister said, "Silly girl, can't you hear him snoring?"

The princesses wrapped golden shawls

around their shoulders and peeked into the room next door.

The oldest whispered, "He's fast asleep." She then said to her youngest sister, "See, there's nothing to worry about. Let's go! The music waits, and so do our dashing dancing partners!"

The oldest sister went over to her bed and tapped on it. A large trap door opened in the floor. A long staircase spiralled down from the opening. Each of the girls climbed down. When the soldier heard the commotion next door, he put on his invisible cloak. He crept into the princesses' room and followed the youngest sister down the stairs. She was always the last one to leave the room.

"Ouch!" she said. "Someone stepped on my dress!"

The soldier quickly lifted his foot. "Silly girl," said one of her sisters. "You've just caught it on a nail. No one stepped on your dress."

When they got to the bottom of the secret stairs, there was a path lined with many trees with leaves of silver. They sparkled in the night. The soldier knew he would need to have proof of this secret world. He reached up and broke off a branch to show the king. It made a large cracking sound.

The youngest daughter heard the noise. She said, "Did you hear that noise? I am sure something's wrong. Maybe we should go back."

"It's just the wind," one of her sisters said. The girls turned down the next path, where the leaves on the trees were made of gold. Then they turned another corner onto a path where the leaves were made of diamonds. Each time they came to a new path, the soldier broke off a branch to show to the king.

The princesses arrived at a lake where twelve princes were waiting for them in twelve boats. The soldier climbed into the boat that carried the youngest princess and her prince. When the boat began moving, her prince said, "Something is strange here. I cannot figure out why the boat is so hard to row tonight."

After rowing for what seemed a long time, they arrived at a distant castle. It was here, the soldier discovered, where all the princesses would dance with their sweethearts. That was how their shoes became worn through. The soldier watched it all happen. The princesses twirled, their beautiful dresses spinning and sparkling in the moonlight.

When it came time to leave, the soldier slipped into the boat with the oldest princess. He knew it would reach the shore first. Once the boat arrived to drop off the girls, he raced back to the castle. When the princesses came back inside, they saw him snoring just as he was before they'd left.

The soldier followed the princesses for the

next two nights. Each evening he took a token from the secret world to show to the king. Not one of the girls ever suspected that the man was following them.

After the third night, the king asked the soldier, "Where do my daughters go each night?"

"They go to a magical palace where they dance all night at a ball with twelve princes," the soldier answered. "They walk through avenues of trees with branches made of silver, gold, and diamonds." He showed the king the branches he had broken off that first night. "Then they travel on a lake to the palace." Then he showed the king the golden cup he had taken from the magic palace.

The king called for his daughters. He asked them if the soldier was telling the truth. When they saw he held the silver, gold, and diamond tree branches, they knew they could not lie to their father. They confessed that the soldier was telling the truth. The king was satisfied. He asked the soldier which of his daughters he would like to marry. The soldier replied, "I am no longer a young man, so perhaps I will marry the eldest."

Their wedding was celebrated with a great ball. There was music and laughter, and the princesses danced the whole night. They wore out their shoes for the very last time.

CHAPTER 11

The Brave Little Tailor

❦

One summer day, a tailor was sewing by his window. He had just bought some delicious jam the day before and was about to enjoy a snack.

"I hope this jam gives me strength and energy," the tailor said. He spread some on a piece of bread. "I'll bet it's delicious! But I will not take a bite until I finish my work on this jacket."

The tailor put the piece of bread and jam down beside him. Sitting back down by his window, he picked up his needle and thread. Flies buzzed all around the bread and jam. He shooed them away. "You're not invited to this party," he said to the flies.

The bugs didn't listen, of course. Soon they were buzzing all around him. The tailor leaped out of his seat and grabbed a rag. He snapped it at the swarm, killing seven flies in one blow.

"Now, that's something!" he said. He finally sat down to eat his bread and jam. He was so proud of himself. To celebrate, he cut the leather for a new belt and embroidered a phrase on it:

Seven in one blow!

The tailor put the belt around his waist and decided to go out into the world to try his luck. He grabbed a piece of old cheese and put it in his pocket. Then he closed up his shop and left. Passing through the city gates, he noticed a bird tangled in a briar bush. He put that into his pocket, too.

He felt brave wearing his new belt and having killed those seven flies. He walked for a long time without getting tired. The road led out of town and to a mountain. He climbed the mountain to the top. There he found a great big giant. But the tailor wasn't afraid. He walked right up to the giant and said, "Greetings, friend. How do you like the view? I'm headed into the world to try my luck. Do you want to come with me?"

The giant looked down at the little man. "Why would I want to go with a small fellow like you?" he asked.

The tailor laughed and unbuttoned his jacket. "See for yourself what a great man I am!" He showed the giant his belt.

The giant read the belt. "Seven in one blow!" he exclaimed. He thought that meant the tailor had killed seven men. "If you're so strong," he said, "can you do this?" The giant picked up a rock and squeezed it so tight that water came running out.

"Is that all?" the tailor replied, laughing. He reached into his pocket and pulled out the wedge of cheese. He squeezed it until all its whey came running out. "Not bad, eh?" he boasted.

The giant could hardly believe his eyes. "What about this!" he said. The giant picked up another rock and threw it very far. In fact, he tossed it so far that neither of them could see it anymore.

"Not bad, not bad," the tailor said. "But watch this! What I throw up into the air will not land anywhere."

He reached into his pocket and pulled out the bird. It was so happy to be free that it flew high up into the sky. Just as the tailor claimed, it didn't fall to earth.

"How's that for a trick?" the tailor said to the giant.

"I will admit that you have a good arm for throwing," the giant said. "But let's see how you can carry things."

The giant walked the tailor down the other side of the mountain. They came to a great forest. The giant stopped in front of a fallen oak tree. "If you're so strong," he said, "you can help me carry this out of the forest."

"I'm at your service," the tailor said. Pointing to the heavy trunk, he added, "Why don't you carry that end? I'll handle all the leaves and branches."

When the giant lifted up the trunk, the tailor hopped onto a branch and rode along. He didn't carry even a leaf. The giant couldn't see behind him, and didn't know he was carrying the tree all by himself. The tailor was having so

much fun. He started to sing. He wanted the giant to believe that lifting the top of the tree was not at all difficult for him. They journeyed a bit farther. Then the giant said, "Let's stop for a second so I can rest."

The tailor quickly hopped off his perch. He ran behind the tree and lifted up the leaves and branches. It looked as if he had been carrying the tree all along. The tailor joked, "A big giant like you? Needing a rest?"

The giant grumbled, "I think we are done with this tree for now."

They left the tree behind and walked on down the road. There was a large cherry tree with beautiful fruit. The giant brought the top branches down so the tailor could grab some. At the very moment the tailor grabbed hold of the fruit, the giant laughed and let go of the tree. The tailor went flying through the air. He rolled when he hit the ground so he wouldn't get hurt.

The giant joked, "What? A big strong tailor like you? Not even able to hold down a cherry branch?"

"I *wanted* to jump over that tree," he said. Challenging the giant, he continued, "A large fellow like yourself shouldn't have any trouble jumping over a tree."

The giant tried to jump over the tree, but he kept getting stuck in the highest branches.

Frustrated, he said to the tailor, "If you're so brave and strong, why don't you try to spend the night in our cave?"

"Sounds like fun," said the tailor.

When they got to the cave, all the giants were eating their dinner. The tailor looked around and said to himself, *Why, there's so much more room here than in my workshop!*

"You must be tired after all the feats you tackled today," the giant said. "I'll show you where you can rest your head."

The giant brought the tailor to a huge bed. "I'm sure you'll be comfortable here," he said. "Good night."

The tailor curled up in one small corner and fell asleep. The giant pretended to go to bed. But he stayed awake until midnight. He kept thinking about how much better the tailor was at all of the things they did that day. The giant grew angry.

"I'll teach him a lesson about who's stronger and more powerful!"

The giant got up and crept over to the tailor's bed. And with a giant iron bar, he swiftly broke the bed in two.

"There," he said. "That should take care of that pesky little fellow for good."

The next morning, the giants woke up and headed out to the forest. The giant told his friends how he had smashed the little tailor's bed the night before. They had soon forgotten about the tailor. Imagine how surprised they were to see him happily skipping along beside the group.

One of them shouted, "It's a trick!"

Another one said, "He must be a ghost!"

"He's come to punish us!" they all screamed at once.

The big giants were so scared of the little tailor. They ran away deep into the forest. The tailor laughed and hopped back onto the road, pleased with himself. "I am so lucky and so brave!" he said.

After a while, he came to a royal courtyard. The grass was green and soft. The tailor decided to lie down and take a nap. A group of people walked by him while he was sleeping. They stopped to read what it said on his belt.

One said aloud, "Seven in one blow!"

Another one said, "What would such a powerful fighter be doing in our peaceful kingdom?"

"We need to see the king right away," they all agreed.

The king sent his deputy out to fetch the tailor. The deputy found him and waited patiently until the tailor woke up.

"The king wishes for you, great warrior, to join the royal army. You will be paid well and you will have a grand place to stay."

"That's exactly why I've come," said the tailor sleepily. "I have come to serve the king."

The deputy brought him back to the palace and showed him to his rooms. The tailor thought to himself, *Why, this is much better than my workshop!*

As the days passed, the king's other soldiers grew more and more afraid of the little tailor.

"What if he turns on us," one of them said, "and strikes seven of us down at a time? We will never survive!"

They told the king that they could no longer be in the same army with such a powerful man. The king did not want to lose his army, but he also didn't want to make the tailor angry. What if he turned on the king? He would strike him down, too. He would take his kingdom. The next morning, the king called for the tailor.

"There are two giants living in my forest, and they are creating many problems. They steal and set fires. My subjects are afraid of them. If you can defeat them, you may marry my daughter. I'll give you half the land in my kingdom."

"At your service, Your Highness," the tailor said. At the same time he was thinking, *A princess to marry and half a kingdom? Now, that's lucky!*

The king said, "I'll send you into the forest with one hundred knights."

The tailor replied, "A man who can manage seven in one blow has little to fear from two giants. I'm sure I will not even need one hundred knights to join me."

The king insisted the tailor set off with the knights anyway. When they reached the edge of the forest, the tailor said to them, "You all can wait here. I can manage this by myself."

The tailor ran as fast as he could into the forest, searching for the giants. At last, he found them snoring under a tree. The tailor gathered many stones and filled up his pockets. Then he climbed the tree.

When he was halfway up, he crawled out on a branch. He was now directly above the slumbering giants. He dropped a stone onto the chest of one. Then he dropped another. After a while, that giant woke up. He noticed all the stones on his chest. The giant shook his friend awake. "Why do you keep throwing stones at me?" he asked.

"You're dreaming," the other giant said. "I haven't thrown anything. I've been sleeping, just like you."

The tailor waited. Both giants went back to sleep. Then he dropped rocks onto the chest of the other giant. That giant woke up and yelled, "What are you doing? Why are *you* now throwing rocks at *me*?"

"I'm not throwing anything! *You* started throwing things!" said the first giant.

The two giants started fighting. They punched, kicked, scratched, and brawled with each other. Soon they knocked themselves out. That's when the tailor shouted for the knights to come. They found the tailor standing next to the fallen giants.

"Hurry and tie them up before they wake up," the tailor said. "Then drag them out of the forest and into the king's jail. They will not cause any more trouble now."

"Aren't you even hurt?" one of the knights asked the tailor.

"Not a scratch," he replied. "They're only two giants. It's not as if I took seven in one blow this time."

The tailor marched back to the king and asked for his promised reward. The king was sorry he'd ever made his promise. He'd never thought the tailor would be able to get rid of two giants at once.

"Before you may marry my daughter and

have half my kingdom," the king said, "you will have to do one more thing for me. You will have to catch a wild boar."

The tailor said, "This will not be a problem. After slaying seven and capturing the giants, catching a boar seems easy enough."

The king sent the tailor out with his royal hunters. When they reached the edge of the forest, the tailor said, "You men can wait here. I'll call out if I need your help."

The royal hunters were happy to be left behind. They had already faced the wild boar a few times. They didn't want to fight it again.

The tailor raced through the woods until he found the boar. It bared its teeth, growled, and ran toward the tailor. The brave little tailor, thinking quickly, jumped into a nearby cabin. The boar followed him inside. The tailor locked the cabin door, leaped out the window, and shut it behind him. The boar was trapped! The tailor laughed and called out to the hunters. They quickly arrived on the scene and saw that he had captured the animal.

Back at the palace, the tailor stood before the king again. He said, "I'm ready for my wedding."

The king had no choice. He had to keep his promise. The brave little tailor had rid his kingdom of two giants and the wild boar.

The tailor married and became a king. He received half of the kingdom as his own. The new king and queen spent many happy days in their kingdom.

One night, the queen heard her husband talking in his sleep. "Boy," he mumbled, "finish up that jacket and hem those pants, or else!"

He's not a warrior! the queen thought. She was shocked. *He's nothing but a lowly tailor*, she realized.

In the morning, the queen went straight to her father and told him everything. She didn't want to be married to a man who was just a tailor. Of course, the king also didn't want the tailor around.

"Here's what I'll do," the king told her. "Open up your bedroom door tonight after he falls asleep. I'll send some knights over to tie him up. We will put him on a ship that's set to sail far away."

"Thank you, Father," the queen said.

After dinner, the tailor and his queen went upstairs to bed. When she thought her husband was sleeping, she quietly got out of bed and opened the door. But one of the knights had overheard the king's plan that day and already told the tailor. The queen didn't know he was only pretending to be asleep.

The queen got back into bed, waiting for the knights to come take her husband away. As the knights arrived at the bedroom door, the tailor shouted, "Boy, finish up that jacket and hem those pants, or else! I've slain seven in one blow, struck down the giants and caught a wild boar. Why would I be afraid of anyone standing outside my bedroom door?"

There were only seven knights standing at the door. They knew they couldn't tie up the mighty tailor. Afraid for their lives, the seven knights ran away and never carried out the king's plan.

The brave, smart, and lucky little tailor smiled to himself in bed. From that moment, no one ever tried to outsmart him again. He lived a long, happy life as king.

What Do *You* Think?
Questions for Discussion

༄

Have you ever been around a toddler who keeps asking the question "Why?" Does your teacher call on you in class with questions from your homework? Do your parents ask you about your day at the dinner table? We are always surrounded by questions that need a specific response. But is it possible to have a question with no right answer?

The following questions are about the book you just read. But this is not a quiz! They are designed to help you look at the people, places, and events in the stories from different angles. These questions do not have specific answers. Instead, they might make you think of the stories in a completely new way.

Think carefully about each question and enjoy discovering more about these classic stories.

1. In some of the fairy tales, such as "The Boy Who Learned Fear," the characters must perform difficult tasks. What do you think are some of the most difficult ones? Which of these tasks might you be able to complete? Which ones would you never even try?

2. In the story "The Worn-Out Dancing Shoes," the king desperately wants to know how his daughters' shoes have become so worn through from dancing. Why do you think he wants to know this so badly? If you were one of the princesses, would you want your secret to be found out? Why, or why not?

3. How is the story "Hansel and Grethel" similar to the story of "Little Brother and Little Sister?" How are the stories different? What is similar about the siblings' relationships in both stories? What is different? What kind of relationship do you have with your siblings?

4. How does Cinderella's life change when her stepmother and stepsisters come to live with her? What do you think her life was like before?

5. In the story "Briar Rose," everyone in the castle falls asleep for many years because of a magic spell. What happens when the people in the castle finally wake up? If you had been asleep for that long, what is the first thing you would want to do when you woke up?

6. The miller's daughter in "Rumpelstiltskin" has to give away the things she values most so the gnome will help her spin straw into gold. How does she feel about having to do this? Is there anything you own that you wouldn't be

willing to give up, even if it meant you would be locked away forever?

7. If you were in the brothers' position in the story "The Golden Goose," would you share your food like Simon does, or would you keep it for yourself? Can you think of a time when you shared something? How did you feel after you shared?

8. In the story "The Brave Little Tailor," the tailor feels he is very lucky. Do you think it was just luck that helped the tailor succeed? Do you think you are a lucky person?

9. In some of the stories, the characters have magical helpers. How do they help the main characters? If you could have a magical friend, what would he or she be like?

10. Do you think the Grimm's fairy tales teach lessons? Are they also fun to read? Did you learn anything from reading these stories?

A Note to Parents and Educators
By Arthur Pober, EdD

⌒

First impressions are important.

Whether we are meeting new people, going to new places, or picking up a book unknown to us, first impressions can count for a lot. They can lead to warm, lasting memories or can make us shy away from future encounters.

Can you recall your own first impressions and earliest memories of reading the classics?

Do you remember wading through pages and pages of text to prepare for an exam? Or were you the child who hid under the blanket to read with a flashlight, joining forces with Robin Hood to save Maid Marian? Do you remember only how long it took you to read a lengthy novel such as *Little Women*? Or did you become best friends with the March sisters?

Even for a gifted young reader, getting through long chapters with dense language can easily become overwhelming and can obscure the richness of the story and its characters. Reading an abridged, newly crafted version of a classic novel can be the gentle introduction a child needs to explore the characters and story line without the frustrations of difficult vocabulary and complex themes.

Reading an abridged version of a classic novel gives the young reader a sense of independence and the satisfaction of finishing a "grown-up" book. And when a child is engaged with and inspired by a classic story, the tone is set for further exploration of the story's themes, characters, history, and details. As a child's reading skills advance, the desire to tackle the original, unabridged version of the story will naturally emerge.

If made accessible to young readers, these stories can become invaluable tools for understanding themselves in the context of their families and social environments. This is why the Classic Starts series includes questions that stimulate discussion regarding the impact and social relevance of the characters and stories today. These questions can foster lively conversations between children and their parents or teachers. When we look at the issues, values, and standards of past times in terms of how we live now, we can appreciate literature's classic tales in a very personal and engaging way.

Share your love of reading the classics with a young child, and introduce an imaginary world real enough to last a lifetime.

Dr. Arthur Pober, EdD

Dr. Arthur Pober has spent more than twenty years in the fields of early childhood and gifted education. He is the former principal of one of the world's oldest laboratory schools for gifted youngsters, Hunter College Elementary School, and former director of Magnet Schools for the Gifted and Talented for more than twenty-five thousand youngsters in New York City.

Dr. Pober is a recognized authority in the areas of media and child protection and is currently the U.S. representative to the European Institute for the Media and European Advertising Standards Alliance.

Explore these wonderful stories in our
Classic Starts™ library.

20,000 Leagues Under the Sea

The Adventures of Huckleberry Finn

The Adventures of Robin Hood

The Adventures of Sherlock Holmes

The Adventures of Tom Sawyer

Alice in Wonderland & Through the Looking Glass

Animal Stories

Anne of Avonlea

Anne of Green Gables

Arabian Nights

Around the World in 80 Days

Ballet Stories

Black Beauty

The Call of the Wild

Dracula

The Five Little Peppers and How They Grew

Frankenstein